The Heart of a Hummingbird

Senyo Adjibolosoo, Ph.D.   Jason Jenkins, MBA

Diane Woods, Illustrator

ISBN: 978-1-948261-04-3

Library of Congress Control Number: 2018931257

Illustrator, Cover and Interior Design: Diane Woods, dianewoodsdesign.com
Interior Layout: Ronda Taylor, heartworkpublishing.com

Hugo House Publishers

Austin, TX • Denver, CO
hugohousepublishers.com

Dedicated to the students of
The Human Factor Leadership Academy.

Grandpa Penni called to Senyo, "My grandson, gather the children. It is time for a story." Grandpa Penni was sitting under the huge Baobab tree, wearing the robe he reserved for special story telling occasions.

Senyo hurried to tell everyone in the village to come to the story tree. No one hesitated. Grandpa Penni did not tell stories often, but when he did, they were always grand.

1

In no time at all, not just the children,
but all the aunties and uncles
in the village had gathered.

Young Senyo prepared the fire. The children helped gather
more wood. When the fire roared, everyone grew quiet.

Grandpa Penni slowly walked over and sat down.
He began to swirl his stick in the fire,
around and around, gathering
his thoughts.

Everyone waited patiently,
listening
to the wind through
the trees and smelling
the sweet smoke
of the fire.

The fire crackled.
Suddenly Grandpa
pushed his stick hard
into the fire, making
the smoke billow up in
clouds above their heads.

Then he began...

3

4

The African
forests and grasslands are
some of the most spectacular places on earth.
This vast land of lush grasses and mighty trees
provides shelter and food to the most remarkable
creatures on earth.

From mighty elephants to
ferocious prides of lions, to the many colorful birds
who breathe the great sacred air of our continent—the land gives
its all so those who live here might thrive.

However, there was a time not too long
ago that a great fire raged on these wild
plains of the African desert.

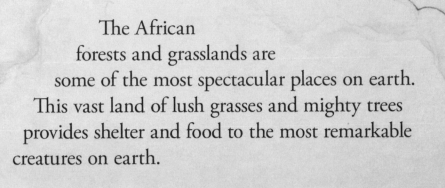

It was a fire the likes of which
had never been witnessed by
any animal or insect.
The flames consumed the
long beautiful grasses
as it travelled
fast over
the land.

It burned as far as the eye could see, and it was so fierce, it forced all the animals in the kingdom into the open. Animals who were once enemies found themselves coming together to survive.

Naturally, they were curious. As they gathered and talked, the same question was asked, "Who started this fire?"

No one knew.

But as the animals kept asking the question the crowd became upset.

Then out of nowhere a small little hummingbird flew onto the scene. He was beautiful with his green and blue feathers shining in the sunlight. He flew far above the crowd, and what he saw shocked him. All the animals in the kingdom were acting crazy chanting the same thing over and over: "Who started the fire?!" "Who started the fire?!"

The hummingbird's fear quickly rose. The fire was growing out of control, and the closer he flew to the group of animals the hotter it became.

The hummingbird realized it didn't matter who started the fire. Instead he knew he needed to do *something* to save his kingdom.

He quickly decided that there was only one who could solve this problem.

The King of Elephants! With his mighty wisdom and legendary strength, surely he would know what to do.

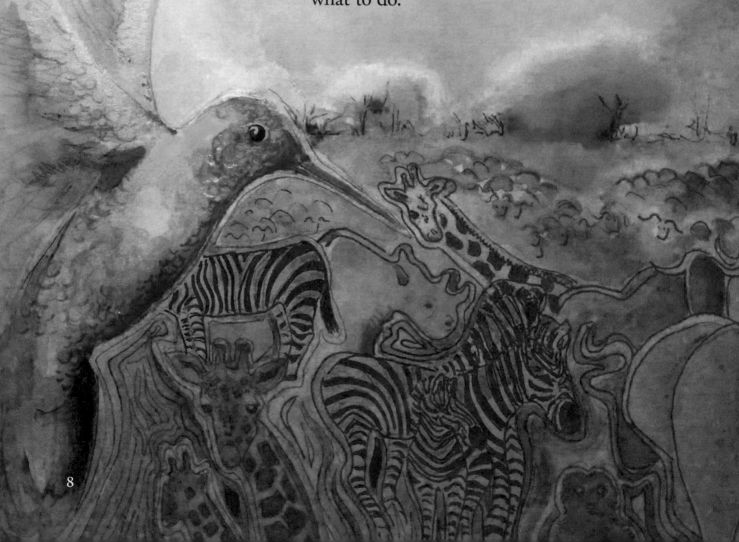

The hummingbird zoomed down. The King and his council were in a tight circle, in a very deep discussion. The hummingbird felt some relief, knowing they would be coming up with a plan to fix this great problem.

"Ahem," the hummingbird cleared his tiny throat.

Nothing. The elephants either didn't hear him or ignored him.

"Excuse me," the hummingbird said, a little louder.

Still no response.

10

Looking over and realizing the fire was closing in on all of them faster than anyone was aware, the hummingbird did something daring. He flew straight into the King's gigantic forehead, poking him right between his eyes with his very sharp beak.

"Ouch! Who dares interrupt this important meeting," King Elephant bellowed, not seeing his attacker immediately, for the bird was so small.

"It was I," the hummingbird said with more courage in his voice than he felt at that moment.

He then even more boldly asked, "King Elephant, what is your plan about putting out this fire?"

King Elephant looked down upon the little bird.

"Hummingbird," King Elephant said in his most superior voice, "you are too small to help! We are trying to find the person who started this fire. When we do, we will deal with them, and then we will focus on putting out the fire."

The hummingbird couldn't quite believe what he was hearing.
This made no sense. Find out who started the fire first?!
How could that possibly help put it out?

The hummingbird became more firm.

"King Elephant, the solution is right in front of us. I
believe if we work together, we can put this fire out."

"We are gathered around a massive lake.
If we work together, as a team, if everyone does their
part, we can do this! We can put out the
fire, and our home will be saved."

King Elephant shot the bird a fierce, ugly look.
Then, without warning,
slammed the tiny bird
to the ground
with
his
mighty
trunk.

14

As the bird lay there stunned,
King Elephant roared, "You fool!
I told you. We are going to find out
who started this fire first, and then we
will put it out!

The hummingbird was dazed and in pain. But after a few minutes he
picked himself up off the ground and flew back to King Elephant.

"We can do this, Sir," the hummingbird shouted. "The solution is
right in front of us."

King Elephant this time smacked the hummingbird with his trunk
so hard that it threw the tiny creature back into the trees
where the fire raged…

As his listeners gasped, Grandpa Penni stopped. He looked around and asked them directly, "Now tell me, my little ones, what do you think of this little bird?"

"Grandpa Penni," one answered, "that bird is not being very smart. He should do what the King wants of him."

"Oh?" Grandpa Penni asked, one eyebrow raised.

"Grandpa Penni, I think that the hummingbird is fearless, and King Elephant is being very mean," Senyo said confidently.

"My children, sometimes it takes great courage to stand up to someone who has power and strength," Grandpa Penni said sternly, "but in life it is your duty to serve others, even when it can seem scary at times."

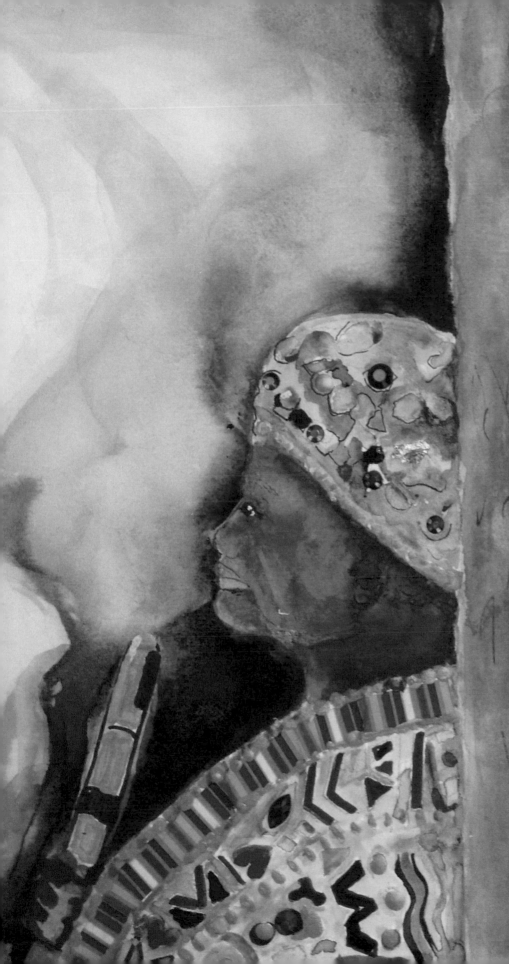

And with that, he threw more wood onto the fire, stirring it around until it had become huge.

It was as if Grandpa wanted the children to experience the same intense heat as the tiny hummingbird.

They quickly moved back a few paces, as Grandpa Penni continued...

17

This hummingbird
was indeed, very brave.
This time, he picked
himself up.

His feathers were ruffled, and he
wasn't able to fly as fast because he was
hurt, but he knew in his heart that he had
to do something.

The hummingbird quickly flew over to the lake. All
the animals thought he was running away.

But the hummingbird had an idea. He flew down and
sucked up as much water as his tiny little beak would hold.

He then
flew up high
into the sky.

The heat was so intense
and the smoke was so
thick he could not see.

When he felt the heat intensify,
he dropped all the water in his
beak.

 It wasn't much. Just a drop.

It evaporated even before it hit the
flames.

The
l i t t l e
bird didn't
care. He flew
back down to the
lake, sucked up as
much water as he could,
then carried it high above the
fire, letting it drop.

As he continued this over and over, a
zebra stopped chanting long enough to
notice.

He nudged his neighbor and pointed with his
nose. "Look at that crazy bird. What do you think
he's doing?"

Others started to notice. "Who does he think he
is?" someone called out. "Does he really think he
can put this fire out? The fire is so big, and he
is so little."

"It's impossible," cried another as
yet another drop of water
evaporated into thin air.

The
little
hummingbird
paid no attention to
what they said. He
didn't seem to notice that
his whole body hurt, that he
was black with smoke and
his once beautiful wings
were burnt almost to
the point that he
couldn't fly.

The second zebra watched that brave little bird fly down to the lake again, suck up another tiny drop of water and release it over the fire. It didn't take long for this zebra to realize that this small creature was risking his life to save not just himself, but all of the animals. He was willing to die instead of just standing by, not doing anything to help.

It was then that this zebra said to himself, "I need to do something, too."

Now this zebra just happened to be the leader of his zebra herd. He ran over to King Elephant.

"Sir, I believe that hummingbird is right. We can put this fire out."

King Elephant began to sputter, "bbut, but who started…"

Before the King could finish, the zebra leader said, "It doesn't matter. What matters is our home. We were wrong, and we must follow the hummingbird. We can put this fire out!" he cried.

And with that, he gathered his herd. They ran to the edge of the fire, and with their swift hooves, kicked dirt onto the flames, stopping the fire from moving any further.

The other animals ran to help. The gigantic horns of the rhinoceroses and strong snouts of the warthogs plowed up more dirt for the deer and gazelles to kick onto the fire.

Even the great cats helped, their strong back legs kicking dirt the farthest.

Massive numbers of birds flew to the lake and sucked up as much water as they could. They then flew right above the flames and dropped what they had stored. You could hear the water singe as it made contact with the fire.

Even the lowly moles figured out that they could tunnel through the ground around the edge of the fire, creating as much a fire break as possible.

As the animals worked, no one noticed the hummingbird drop to a rock, completely exhausted. He could no longer fly, but that didn't stop him from cheering on the fight. The animals could hear his little voice shouting, "You can do it. Keep fighting this fire!"

His spirit encouraged the animals to fight even harder.

King Elephant gathered his tribe, and together they thundered down to the water's edge.

As one, they sucked up water in their mighty trunks, and as quickly as they could, blew that water over the fire.

The battle raged for many days and nights, but together the animals saved their home.

Black, charred earth was everywhere. In the distant horizon, welcome thunder clouds were beginning to churn. Soon, the healing power of rain would help restore the forest and grasslands to their breathtaking glory.

King Elephant was completely exhausted and burned from battling the flames. But he knew he had one more important task at hand.

He looked and looked...and finally found what he wanted. There, on a rock close to the lake, lay the little bird. He had not moved.

When the mighty King Elephant spotted the bird, a huge wave of emotion washed over him. Choking back tears, he lumbered over to where the tiny bird lay. And very gently, with much fanfare, lifted his brave new friend and let him rest on his massive head.

"Animals of this kingdom," King Elephant thundered so everyone could hear. "I proclaim this little hummingbird the hero and savior of our land."

All the animals cheered.

"Oh no," the hummingbird protested. "It wasn't I who put out the fire. It was all of you, and if it were not for the elephants," he said, looking all around him, "then we would not be here."

"Ahem." It was King Elephant's turn to interrupt the bird. "If it were not for you, my courageous friend, we would have died trying to find something, or someone, to blame, and that would not have done anything to extinguish the flames."

"Thank you," the hummingbird humbly said, as all of the animals once again cheered on and on. Their home was saved, and they had learned how important it was to work together, no matter how big or small.

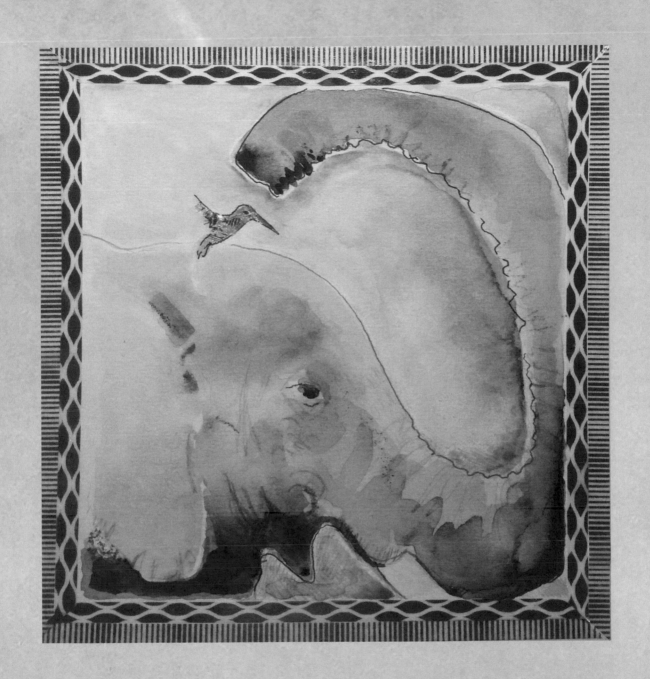

Grandpa Penni grew quiet and stared sternly into the fire. Finally, a little girl said, "Grandpa Penni, I think what the hummingbird did was very important. He stood up to the big elephants and did what was right even though no one believed in him."

"That is right child," Grandpa Penni said knowingly. "Remember this, no matter what the fire is in our lives, we must do something. For to do nothing will only let it burn, and that fire will eventually destroy us."

"And," he continued, "no matter how small you are and how impossible the task may seem, it is you who can make a difference."

Grandpa Penni paused, looking intently at each person who had gathered as he continued to swirl his stick in the fire.

"Perhaps most importantly," he finally said,

"It is my desire,

that when you are called,

you, too,

will have

the heart

of a hummingbird."

As he finished his story, he looked again into the eyes of each child, and as he went from face to face, his own lit up with a most magnificent smile.

For he knew they understood.

Dear Parents, Teachers, Kids—anyone who has read this story:

This story has for many years touched us in so many ways, and we have found so many layers of rich meaning in it. Senyo learned the story as a young boy, sitting around a campfire in Ghana, and Jason was told the story when he was meeting with hundreds of Ghanian teachers. We have often thought of the hummingbird at times when we needed to be brave—or to let go of preconceived ideas about what we thought was right when it wasn't. So we want to have you have a chance to reflect on how this story can touch your life.

Below are seven questions with space to write your answers. There are no right or wrong answers to any of them.

Ask them of each other. Discuss them. Come back to them later—even years from now—to see if your answer still holds or if your viewpoint has changed.

My wish is that you find the *Heart of a Hummingbird* as much a touchstone in your life as it has been mine. And may your life be richer for it!

1. The fire in this story can be symbolic (meaning it can represent an idea) of any difficulty or hardship you are facing in your life. What is the "fire" in your life right now? Discuss how your "fire" may feel like it's so overwhelming, you think you don't know what to do.

2. How many times in your life have you had to deal with someone like King Elephant? His pride and arrogance almost killed everyone. Discuss times where you looked for ways to solve a problem, but what you came up with didn't help. Then discuss a time when you did find the reason for a problem and the problem was then able to be handled. Which one works better?

3. Go back to your "fire." Is there an "elephant," who you think is too important or too "big" for you to talk to, to handle the issue, because you think you are too "insignificant."

4. The zebra has a small but very important role in this story. He is able to see quickly and clearly what the hummingbird is doing. Discuss times when you have seen people being a Zebra-type character, one who was willing to go against what everyone else thought. How willing were others to join in what this person was trying to get others to do? If there was resistance, discuss why. Or discuss why people were willing to follow that "voice of reason," over what the leaders were wanting to do.

5. The hummingbird is an amazing creature. Discuss the ways he is courageous and why he might be that way.

6. The hummingbird didn't care that he was "too small," or not "powerful enough" to make a difference. He realized that doing something was far better than doing nothing to put out the fire. Discuss a time in your life when you decided to do something, even though it might seem like it wouldn't make any difference. What happened? How did that make you feel?

7. Go back to the "fire" in your life you identified in question #1. How can you be like the hummingbird and find ways to handle that problem?

Thank you for taking the time to think about and discuss these questions. We hope that they help you see how you, too, can have the heart of a hummingbird, no matter what obstacles you face in your life.

Senyo Adjibolosoo
Jason Jenkins

Why The Human Factor Leadership Academy

The Human Factor Leadership Academy (HFLA) is a school in Akatsi, a small city in Ghana. It is in the Volta region of that wonderful country, and it is where the "Heart of the Hummingbird" story has been told for generations, much like the way it is told in this book.

The school was established in 2005 to help bring hope in the most sustainable way. History has proven over and over as to what that solution is: it's something we call *"foundational leadership."* It fosters the development of leadership characteristics through world-class education. It is making sure that the investment between the heart and mind are equally balanced and strongly connected.

Foundational leadership's core characteristics are: honesty, trust, integrity, compassion, service, vision, and relevant knowledge and skills.

We have found that when these leadership characteristics are properly learned and applied, the seed of change is being watered and the environment for change can flourish in the lives of all those who call Africa home. But this school also brings opportunity for all of us, for the HFLA is already touching lives in multiple countries. The demand for the curriculum has been overwhelming, and its future is bright.

The Academy today is a thriving school for grades nursery school through senior high school and plans are in place to expand the school to a full-fledged accredited university. Currently, there are over 650 full-time students on a campus that sits on thirty acres. It contains an excellent library in downtown Akatsi that will expand over time and there is full transportation from town to the school campus.

We have made an impact, but bringing our vision to full fruition cannot be accomplished alone. We published this book for two main reasons:

1. **Impact you and your family's lives:**
   We hope you found beauty in this story and that it has enriched your life and the lives of those around you. It contains many great principles for all of us to reflect on and apply.

2. **Share our vision and ask for your help:**
   It is our desire that we find others who want to help support the Human Factor Leadership Academy and other organizations that are focused on delivering sustainable solutions that make the world we all live in better.

Please visit **www.iihfd.org** and/or **https://www.facebook.com/HFLAIIHFD** to learn more about how you can get involved with this project. There are many avenues for you to help that go beyond just monetary support.

Lastly, we deeply appreciate your support in purchasing this book. Proceeds go to support The Human Factor Leadership Academy, and we look forward to your continued support.

Sincerely,

Senyo & Jason

About the Authors

Senyo Adjibolosoo, Ph.D., is from Ghana, Africa and is an accomplished scholar and author. A professor of economics at Point Loma Nazarene University and a Distinguished Toastmaster, Dr. Adjibolosoo has published numerous books and articles, is a life-long educator, ordained Reverend Minister, Church Planter, motivational speaker, and a Master-Class teacher in Spiritual Formation. He writes inspirational poetry, conducts seminars on Marriage Enrichment, and is the founder of the Institute for Human Factor Development (IIHFD).

Jason Jenkins, MBA, is the creator and CEO of proprietary portfolio monitoring asset-protection system, AssetLock. An accomplished author and accomplished speaker, Jenkins has won numerous business award including The 2015 American Business Awards Gold Stevie® Winner for Financial Services TechStartup of the Year, and the 2015 CEO World Awards Gold Winner for Financial Services & Banking Startup of the Year. In 2014, he was honored by Retirement Advisor Magazine as the "Advisor of the Year." He helped found the Human Factor Leadership Academy with Dr. Senyo Adjibolosoo.

Notes

Notes

Notes

Notes

Notes